Fifty-five Grandmas and a Llama

words by Lynn Manuel · pictures by Carolyn Fisher

GIBBS·SMITH
PUBLISHER

First edition

99 98 97 5 4 3 2 1

Text copyright © 1997 by Lynn Manuel

Illustration copyright © 1997 by Carolyn Fisher

This is a Peregrine Smith book, published by

Gibbs Smith, Publisher

P.O. Box 667

Layton, Utah 84041

Book design by Steven Arthur

Printed and bound in China

Library of Congress Cataloging-in-Publication Data

Manuel, Lynn.

Fifty-five grandmas and a llama / by Lynn Manuel; illustrated by Carolyn Fisher.

p.   cm.

Summary: Sam's efforts to find a grandmother are so successful that he discovers the
problems of having too many grandmothers.

ISBN 0-87905-785-8

[1. Grandmothers–Fiction.]

I. Fisher, Carolyn Noelle, 1968–ill.

II. Title.

PZ7.M3192FI 1997

[E]–dc20

96-29473

CIP

AC

To David. May all your wishes come true.

L.M.

For my grandmas, Olive Fisher and Lois Conrad.

C.F.

Sam lived with his mother in a little house by the sea. Most of the time Sam was happy. But there was something he wanted very much.

"I wish I had a grandma," Sam said. "I wish it more than anything."

Sam wished for a grandma when he saw the first star at night. He wished for a grandma when he blew out the candles on his birthday cake. He wished for a grandma when he got the wishbone at Christmas.

Sam wished and wished and wished. Then one day, he asked his mother, "Do wishes ever come true?"

"Sometimes," said his mother. "But you must do something to make your wishes come true."

Sam nodded his head. "I will find out where I can get a grandma."

Sam took all the dimes and nickels from his piggy bank. He thought a grandma might cost a bit of money. Then Sam hurried down the street.

He waited at the corner for the light to change. Sam saw a firefighter on a ladder. The firefighter was bringing a cat down from a tree.

"Excuse me," Sam said to the firefighter, "do you know where I can get a grandma?"

"No." The firefighter tickled the kitten under the chin. The kitten purred. "Grandmas do not grow on trees, you know."

"Thanks anyway," said Sam.

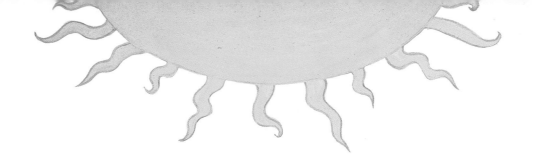

Sam passed a store. There was a sign in the window: *We sell everything under the sun.*

"Excuse me," Sam said to the lady behind the counter. "Do you know where I can get a grandma?"

"No." The lady dusted the counter. The dust made her sneeze. "Grandmas are not a dime a dozen, you know."

"Thanks anyway," said Sam.

Sam stopped in the park. He saw a magician with a black hat and a black cape. The magician made the children laugh and clap their hands.

"Excuse me," Sam said to the magician. "Do you know where I can get a grandma?"

"No." The magician pulled a white rabbit out of his hat. The rabbit hopped all around the children. "You cannot pull grandmas out of hats, you know."

"Thanks anyway," said Sam.

Sam frowned. Grandmas did not grow on trees. Grandmas were not a dime a dozen. And grandmas could not be pulled out of hats. So where could he get a grandma?

Then Sam had an idea. He turned in at the newspaper office. They had all the news. They would tell him where he could get a grandma.

Sam stood in line behind a man with white hair.

"I want to put something in the paper," the man said.

"What would you like to say?" asked the lady in charge.

The man said, "'Gentleman looking for nice lady to go for long walks and talks.'"

The lady wrote it down on a pad of paper. The man paid the lady and left.

It was Sam's turn next. "Hello," said Sam. He put his money on the counter. He put the nickels in one pile. He put the dimes in another pile.

"Oh, hello," said the lady. "What would you like to say?"

Sam said, "'Very nice boy looking for grandma who likes to do grandma things.'"

The lady wrote it down. "Good luck," she said.

Sam waited and waited. Then one day the phone rang. It was the newspaper lady.

"You must come to the office right away!" she said.

Sam zoomed down the street and zipped through the park. He could smell lavender in the air. When he turned right at the corner, he saw the grandmas. They were lined up all the way from the corner to the newspaper office!

"I can't believe it!" Sam said to the lady in charge. "I have never seen so many grandmas!"

"I think there are fifty-five," said the lady. "But the grandmas keep moving. They are hard to count."

Sam went out to count them.

There were ten grandmas with cats that meowed.

There were nine grandmas singing like meadowlarks.

There were eight grandmas knitting socks.

There were seven grandmas with flour on their noses.

There were six grandmas wearing garden gloves.

There were five grandmas waving lace hankies.

There were four grandmas snapping photos.

There were three grandmas eating pickles.

There were two grandmas with bluey-white hair.

And there was one grandma wearing a black leather jacket. This grandma had a llama!

The lady in charge said, "What are you going to do with fifty-five grandmas and a llama?"

"Keep them!" said Sam. "You can never have too many grandmas!"

Sam led a line of grandmas and a llama down the street. He thought his grandmas were the most beautiful grandmas in the world!

The little house by the sea spilled over with grandmas.

When they sat down to dinner, the grandmas watched Sam.

"Sam eats like a bird!"

"Sam needs more fat on his bones!"

"Eat your greens, dear!"

"A pickle a day keeps the doctor away!"

The grandma with the llama just winked and smiled.

When Sam went to bed, the grandmas came up to say good night. One by one, they tucked him in. They tucked and tucked and tucked. Sam tried to wiggle his toes, but they would not budge.

The grandma with the llama just winked and smiled.

The next morning, Sam took his fifty-five grandmas and a llama to school for show-and-tell. Everyone said Sam was very lucky!

Before the grandmas left, they gave Sam a hug. They hugged and hugged and hugged. Sam was squished! The class giggled, and Sam turned red.

The grandma with the llama just winked and smiled.

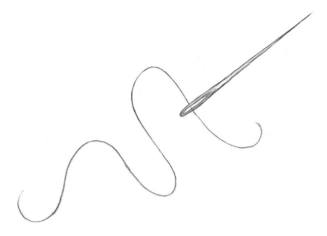

After school, the grandmas stuck with Sam. They stuck like glue. When Sam went for a bike ride, the grandmas were right behind him. When Sam put a hole in the knee of his pants, the grandmas chased after him with darning needles.

The grandma with the llama just winked and smiled.

When Sam made a little sniffling sound, the grandmas carried him into the house.

"Sam has a chill!"

"Sam needs lots of bed rest!"

"Call a doctor!"

In a flash, Sam was tucked into bed. A grandma closed the top button of his green shirt. A grandma pulled a red knitted cap over his ears. And another grandma put thick wool socks on his feet.

But Sam did not feel sick. He wanted to play with the other boys and girls. When the grandmas closed the door behind them, Sam slipped out of bed. He went to the window.

Everywhere he looked, he saw a grandma.

One grandma was sitting on the llama and smiling up at him.

Two grandmas were knitting lace covers for the garbage cans.

Three grandmas were planting lavender plants.

Four grandmas were square dancing on the grass.

Five grandmas were snapping pictures of the cats.

Six grandmas were singing about peanut-butter cookies.

Seven grandmas were napping in the tree house.

Eight grandmas were painting pickle pictures.

Nine grandmas were playing bingo.

Ten grandmas were on the way upstairs to hug him.

The grandmas hugged and hugged and hugged!

As soon as they had gone, Sam slipped away. He knew what he had to do.

Sam ran all the way to the newspaper office. He ran so hard that he was puffing!

"I made a big mistake!" Sam said to the lady in charge. "You *can* have too many grandmas!"

"Everybody makes mistakes," said the lady.

Sam put his money on the counter. He put the nickels in one pile. He put the dimes in another pile.

"What would you like to say this time?" asked the lady.

Sam thought. Then he said, "'Nice grandmas looking for very nice boys and girls.'"

The lady said, "Good luck."

Gentleman looking for nice lady to go for long walks and talks. Must like dogs. Reply w/photo to PO Box T, The Journal.

WANTED: Nice grandmas looking for very nice boys and girls. Send applications to PO Box F, The Journal.

One day Sam looked out his window. A long line of boys and girls was marching down the street. They were coming to get a grandma!

The little house by the sea was bursting at the seams. Grandmas and boys and girls were everywhere! They were hanging out of windows and sitting on the stairs. They were swinging from the apple tree and singing on the roof. Everybody ate pickles and peanut-butter cookies. It was the best party in the whole world!

When it was almost dark, they began to leave. Some grandmas left with girls. Some grandmas left with boys. Some grandmas left with boys and girls. And one grandma left with a white-haired man. It was the man from the newspaper office who wanted a nice lady to go for walks and talks!

The grandmas patted Sam on the head as they went past. "You will always have a special place in our hearts," they said to Sam. And then they waved good-bye.

"It was lots of fun!" Sam called after them.

Soon the little house by the sea was quiet and still. Sam went outside and sat under the apple tree. He thought to himself, "First I do not have any grandmas, then I have too many. And now I do not have any again."

Sam closed his eyes. He felt sad.

Suddenly he heard a twig snapping. He opened one eye. He opened the other eye. It was the grandma with the llama! She winked and smiled at Sam.

Sam and his grandma went to the corner to get some ice cream. And the llama had chocolate ripple.